Life in the  New American Nation™

The War of 1812

The New American Nation Goes to War with England

Mark Beyer

rosen central
Primary Source™

The Rosen Publishing Group, Inc., New York

To the memory of our nation's founding fathers, who looked further than self-interest

Published in 2004 by The Rosen Publishing Group, Inc.
29 East 21st Street, New York, NY 10010

Library of Congress Cataloging-in-Publication Data

Beyer, Mark (Mark T.)
The War of 1812: the new American nation goes to war with England / by Mark Beyer.
    v. cm. — (Life in the new American nation)
Includes bibliographical references (p.) and index.
Contents: The causes for war—America fights—The British attack Washington, DC—A peace treaty and war's end.
ISBN 0-8239-4043-8 (lib. bdg.)
ISBN 0-8239-4261-9 (pbk. bdg.)
6-pack ISBN 0-8239-4274-0
1. United States—History—War of 1812—Juvenile literature. [1.United States—History—War of 1812.] I. Title. II. Series.
E354 .B49 2003
973.5'2—dc21

2002156103

Manufactured in the United States of America

cover (left): Treaty of Ghent, 1814
cover (right): The Battle of New Orleans and the death of Major General Packenham

Photo credits: cover photos (left), pp. 5, 15, 23 (top and bottom), 24 © National Archive and Records Administration; cover photos (right), pp. 1, 18, 20 courtesy of Library of Congress; pp. 6, 10 © Bettmann/Corbis; p. 9 © AP/World Wide Photos; p. 12 © Stapleton Collection/Corbis; pp. 16, 26 © Hulton/Archive/Getty Images.

Designer: Nelson Sá; Editor: Eliza Berkowitz; Photo Researcher: Nelson Sá

Contents

Introduction

Today the United States and Great Britain are friends. They were not always friendly, however. More than 200 years ago, the United States fought Great Britain in the Revolutionary War (1775–1783). This war was the United States's fight to gain independence. Twenty-nine years later, the two nations fought again. In 1812, the United States attacked British forts in Canada. This started what came to be known as the War of 1812. This war lasted until 1815 and included American and British soldiers, Canadians, African American slaves, and First Nations Native Americans. The First Nations were the original group of Native Americans recognized by the Canadian government.

The arguments that caused the War of 1812 went all the way back to 1793. In that year, Britain and France started a war against each other. They fought a lot of this war at sea, using warships. This war

This print of the Battle of Lexington was created by John Baker in 1882. The Battle of Lexington began in 1775 and marked the beginning of the United States Revolutionary War. This war went on until 1783.

made merchant shipping difficult. All of Europe and the new United States had trouble bringing their goods to foreign ports. The United States was angry because most of its income came from merchant shipping. President George Washington and President John Adams helped to ease the anger, and shipping problems lessened.

By 1805, French emperor Napoléon Bonaparte and his people ruled much of Europe. Britain still ruled the

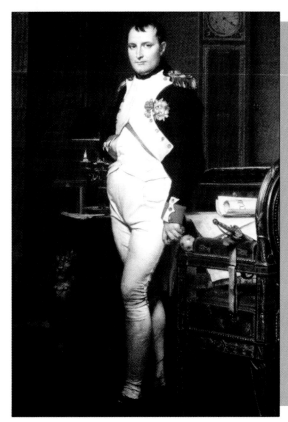

This painting of Napoléon Bonaparte was created by Jacques-Louis David in 1812. Napoléon was emperor of France for about ten years. During his time in power, he led France in a war against the British. He eventually lost power and was sent to live on a faraway island.

seas with its powerful navy. Britain began to blockade all European ports to fight the French. It also captured merchant ships. Once again, the United States was caught in the middle. It began losing goods, money, ships, and men. The British navy kidnapped American sailors and forced them to work on British warships. This practice greatly angered the U.S. government. Between 1803 and 1812, British naval captains forced more than 10,000 American citizens to work on British ships.

The Causes for War — Chapter 1

Meanwhile, America grew quickly after the Revolutionary War. The settlers needed land. Since the end of the war, the U.S. government had urged the settlers to move west and north. Canada was in the north and had rich hunting and farming areas. British forts protected Canadians in Quebec City, Montreal, and York (now called Toronto). Between the United States and Canada lay the First Nations Indian land.

In the West, the American government paid cash for land. It also signed treaties with the First Nations for the use of the land in other places. America wanted to use the whole territory for its growing population. It also wanted to push the

The American government had been upset with the British since the end of the Revolutionary War in 1783. The British had not retreated from American territory all across the Great Lakes (from northern New York to Detroit). Worse, the British backed Native Americans in their fight to hold onto their lands all around the American frontiers. This was made worse by Britain's refusal to trade fairly with the Americans after the war. The stage was set for another war in the future. Twenty-nine years after the end of their first war, the Americans got their chance for revenge. The War of 1812 was partly based on arguments of the past.

British military out of North America. The U.S. government needed a plan to do both. The British and French blockade of Europe helped its plan.

The United States decided to start a war with the British. Americans were unhappy that their merchant shipping suffered and American citizens were forced to work on British ships. The United States knew it could attack Canada, seize land, and get rid of the British all at the same time. Three events set the war in motion. In June 1807, the British warship *Leopard* fired on the American ship *Chesapeake* off the shores of Norfolk, Virginia. The *Chesapeake's* sailors had refused to allow the British to board their ship. Three Americans died in the attack.

Constitution & Guerriere

This is an etching showing a British and an American ship in a battle during the War of 1812. The British ship, *Guerriere* (*left*), was destroyed by the United States's ship, *Constitution* (*right*), after only thirty minutes.

In 1810, the War Hawks were elected to Congress. These were a group of men outraged by British acts of piracy and war against the United States. They stirred up anger in Congress and with Americans towards Britain. They demanded that President James Madison do something to defend the country.

This is an image of the Battle of Tippecanoe, which occurred on November 7, 1811. Native American and American soldiers fought this battle at Prophetstown, which is near modern-day Lafayette, Indiana. Though both sides lost the same amount of people, it was considered a victory for the United States.

Finally, in 1811 in the Ohio River Valley, a Native American leader named the Prophet attacked an American army force at Tippecanoe. The War Hawks blamed the British for stirring up trouble with the Native Americans. They now called on President Madison to ask Congress for a declaration of war.

America Fights   Chapter 2

In 1810, United States citizens elected a new Congress. By then the economy had been hurt by Napoléon's European war and the British blockade. The shippers and textile manufacturers in New England were almost broke. Southern farmers had nowhere to sell their produce overseas. And Native Americans were attacking settlers all over the American frontier. Something had to be done.

The War Hawks, led by John C. Calhoun of South Carolina, wanted Congress to declare war against Britain. They argued that invading Canada and attacking British forts would change Britain's trade rules and save the country from financial ruin. At the same time, the United States would rid itself of British forces on the continent. This would also gain land for the growing nation.

On June 18, 1812, Congress passed a declaration of war against Britain. They thought that the British would be too worried about their war with France to care what happened in the Canadian colonies. Madison, the War Hawks, and the military generals thought Britain would quickly ask for peace so they could stay focused on France. The Americans were wrong. One problem was that American military forces were not prepared to fight.

This print of John C. Calhoun was created around 1860. Calhoun was the leader of the War Hawks, a group that encouraged war with Britain. Later in his life, Calhoun became the seventh vice president of the United States.

They had too few fighting men and ships. They thought that the Canadian colonists and the Native Americans would be on their side. But, facing death and takeover by the American government, these two groups helped defend their cities against the Americans. American forces thought they would have to battle only British troops. They were surprised to find that French Canadians and First Nations Indians backed the British.

American military forces planned to attack Canada in three places. In the west, General William Hull would attack from Detroit and march across upper Canada. A force at the Niagara River in the center of the Great Lakes would take Queenston Heights. In the east, forces at Lake Champlain (in upper New York) planned to take Montreal. The attacks were poorly planned and each failed.

The War Hawks Versus the Federalists

The War Hawks represented farming interests of western and southern states. They belonged to the Democratic-Republican political party. This group believed that each state should have its own government, and they were in favor of war with Britain. On the other hand, the Federalists represented New England shippers and manufacturers. They thought war would help ruin New England shipping. In the end, the War Hawks convinced Congress to declare war.

The Other Constitution

The American warship *Constitution* became famous during the War of 1812. The *Constitution* was fitted with metal plates on its sides to repel cannonballs. It gained the nickname "Old Ironsides" after a British sailor saw cannonballs bouncing off its iron plates. The *Constitution* never lost a sea battle.

Hull surrendered the city of Detroit to British forces on August 18, 1812. At Queenston Heights in October, half the American troops fought up the steep sides of the bluffs to the heights. The other half refused to cross the Niagara River when they saw that the fighting was so fierce on the other side. British reinforcements finally surrounded the small American force on the Canadian side of the river. At the end of the year across the Lake Champlain front, short battles forced the American forces to retreat quickly. They barely fought before running away.

The only American forces to do well in that first year were the American navy ships. They won several single-ship battles up and down the East Coast. These successes were few and short lived, however. The British navy began a blockade of the United States coastline. American hopes that the

Early on in the War of 1812, William Hull, governor of the Michigan Territory, surrendered the city of Detroit to the British. This document, signed by Hull and others, was dated August 16, 1812. Hull gave up his army and his forts to the British.

CAMP at DETROIT 16 August 1812.

CAPITULATION for the Surrender of Fort Detroit entered into between Major General Brock, commanding His Britannic Majesty's forces, on the one part, & Brigadier General Hull, commanding the North-Western Army of the United-States on the other part.

1st. Fort Detroit, with all the troops, regulars as well as Militia, will be immediately Surrendered to the British forces under the Command of Maj. Gen. Brock, & will be considered prisoners of war, with the exception of such of the Militia of the Michigan Territory who have not joined the Army.

2d. All public Stores, arms & all public documents including every thing else of a public nature will be immediately given up.

3d. Private Persons & property of every description shall be respected.

4th. His excellency Brigadier Gen. Hull having expressed a desire that a detachment from the State of Ohio, on its way to join his Army, as well as one sent from Fort Detroit, under the Command of Colonel McArthur, should be included in the above Capitulation, it is accordingly agreed to. It is however to be understood that such part of the Ohio - Militia, as have not joined the Army, will be permitted to return to their homes, on condition that they will not serve during the war; their arms however will be delivered up, if belonging to the public.

5th. The Garrison will march out at the hour of twelve o'clock, & the British forces will take immediately possession of the Fort.

APPROVED.
(Signed) W. HULL, Brigr.
Genl.Comg. the N.W.Army.

APPROVED.
(Signed) ISAAC BROCK,
Major General.

(Signed.) J. McDonell Lieut.
Col. Militia. P. A. D. C.
J. B. Glegg Major A. D. C.
James Miller Lieut. Col.
5th. U. S. Infantry.
E. Brush Col. Comg. 1st. Regtt.
Michigan Militia.

A true Copy.

ROBERT NICHOL Lieut. Coit
& Qr. M. Genl. Militia.

British would be occupied with their French war were crushed. American coastal cities soon found themselves attacked by more powerful and experienced warriors.

In 1813, American forces attacked Canada for a second time. Once again, they attacked in three places. The east and central forces were beaten at Niagara and

On September 10, 1813, commander Oliver Hazard Perry's ships defeated a fleet of British ships. This lithograph by Nathaniel Currier shows the United States's nine ships battling Britain's six ships on Lake Erie, Michigan.

Montreal after fierce fighting. Only in the west did American forces succeed. Detroit was retaken, and the region was secured. In Lake Erie, Oliver Hazard Perry's ships sank the British fleet on September 10, 1813. This would be the last of American successes for a long time. Britain was winning its war with Napoléon in Europe. France was collapsing. Now the British turned westward and sailed across the Atlantic.

The British Attack Washington, D.C.

Chapter 3

As 1814 began, the American army and navy faced defeat. The British navy had more than a thousand ships. They also had an experienced army. The French were now defeated, and the British sent men and ships to the American coast. There they began to attack any American ship setting sail from seaports. The British also stopped any foreign ships from entering American ports. This blockade damaged the American economy. People, merchants, and the government were nearly out of money.

Britain saw a great advantage in America's failing economy and weak military. They planned to attack the United States mainland, thinking this would force President Madison and the U.S. Congress to ask for peace. When this happened, the British could then expect to get huge amounts of North American land in exchange for peace.

The British had orders to "destroy and lay waste" to the American army and navy. The British planned their own naval and land attacks during the summer of 1814. In the north, they wanted to separate New England from the rest of the country. To do this, they attacked up the Hudson River and on Lake Champlain. On the seaboard they attacked

This portrait of James Madison, the fourth president of the United States, was painted by Gilbert Stuart. It was believed to have been created in 1828. Madison was president during the War of 1812.

in Chesapeake Bay near Washington, D.C. They also attacked New Orleans from the sea to block shipping up the Mississippi River.

President Madison feared that Washington, D.C., was not ready to defend itself. He was right. British forces sailed up the Chesapeake and fought their way into Washington. Madison and his government fled to Virginia. The British stormed into the capital and burned the White House, the Capitol, and other government buildings. They set the city ablaze, but a hard rainstorm saved Washington from burning to the ground.

At this point, the American army and navy turned the tide of the war. The British forces in Washington moved to take Baltimore. The battle at Fort McHenry

Early Peace Talks Fail

Peace was never out of the question during the War of 1812. The United States tried to settle the war with Britain several times. It asked Britain to promise not to kidnap American sailors. It also wanted to help settle Native American claims along the Canadian border. Lastly, it wanted to begin fair trade practices. These were the original disputes that had fueled the start of the war. Talks between the warring countries failed until November 1814.

This is a wood engraving from the early 1800s. It shows Washington, D.C., during the attack by British military forces on August 24, 1814. If it were not for a rainstorm, Washington, D.C., might have been destroyed by fire that day.

turned the British back. This battle inspired Francis Scott Key to write the "Star-Spangled Banner." British forces had been defeated in the heart of America.

Meanwhile, 10,000 British soldiers attacked America in the north from Montreal. This battle proved to be the key to ending the war hostilities. The British planned to defeat the American navy on Lake Champlain and then take New York City. American captain Thomas MacDough defeated the British navy at Plattsburg Bay on September 11, 1814. The British then retreated into Canada.

The British government saw that it was best to stop the war. It wanted to settle its arguments with America. Its army and navy were tired from so many years of fighting the French. Likewise, its government was as starved for money as the Americans. It was time to stop fighting.

African American Sailors

As in the American Revolution, African Americans fought for their country during the War of 1812. The U.S. Navy asked Congress to let it use African American sailors. In 1813, Congress passed an act to allow this. African American sailors fought in the major naval battles of the war, including on Lake Erie and Lake Champlain, and the Battle of New Orleans. African American sailors hoped their service would help prove to the government that they deserved equal rights and freedom.

Chapter 4

A Peace Treaty and War's End

After the British attacks failed in the summer of 1814, Britain offered peace with the Americans. President Madison gladly accepted. In November 1814, British and American negotiators met in Ghent, Belgium.

From the beginning, what America had wanted most was for the British navy to stop bothering American shipping. The war had begun because of trade disputes. If trade could start again without trouble, peace would be easily had. America made Britain promise not to kidnap American sailors. Oddly, this was no longer an issue. Since the French defeat, Britain had too many sailors.

The end of the War of 1812 was marked by the signing of the Treaty of Ghent. The Treaty of Ghent *(right)* was signed on December 24, 1814. The signing of the treaty *(bottom)* officially put an end to the War of 1812, although the fighting continued until February 1815. This was because it took a while for the news that the war had ended to reach the soldiers.

The British had one main issue to solve, too. They wanted to create a Native American territory between Canada and the United States. This was a promise to the Native Americans that dated back to the Revolutionary War. The British saw this as a chance to

This is a copy of an engraving depicting the Battle of New Orleans. This battle was fought after the War of 1812 had officially ended. News of the treaty had not yet reached New Orleans, where American and British soldiers continued fighting.

help the First Nations Indians and create a buffer zone. This zone would separate American and British forces so no more hostilities would happen.

The Americans didn't like this idea at all. In fact, it was the one point that they were willing to continue fighting over. They felt that these lands were theirs to buy or contract to live on from the Native Americans. Already, hundreds of American settlers farmed on these lands. Native Americans had also attacked them for years. American negotiators told Britain that America needed these lands. They wouldn't budge on this point.

Peace treaty talks almost broke down. American negotiators threatened to walk out. They did this to see if the British would back down on their Native American issues. The British decided finally that

New Orleans: News of Peace Comes Too Late

Almost 200 years ago, news was slow to travel. As the two sides discussed peace in Belgium, the Battle of New Orleans wore on. Two weeks after Britain and America signed the Treaty of Ghent, the Battle of New Orleans finally ended with a powerful land battle. General Andrew Jackson defeated the British at Chalmette, helping the Americans win the largest battle of the war—after the war was officially over!

helping the Native Americans wasn't that important. America and Britain signed the Treaty of Ghent on Christmas Eve 1814. The treaty addressed eleven points of interest. These points stated that America and Britain would stop fighting on land and at sea.

A BOXING MATCH, or Another Bloody Nose for JOHN BULL.

This political cartoon from 1813 shows President James Madison giving King George III of Great Britain a bloody nose. This is a reflection of how the United States felt about Great Britain during the War of 1812.

Land won during the war by either nation would be given back. Finally, a commission would be created to settle border disputes.

Many people in both the American and British governments thought the Treaty of Ghent would not last. They saw border disputes as the biggest problem. Britain wanted to expand its Canadian lands. America had already been expanding its lands. But unlike many countries throughout history, Great Britain and American never fought another war against each other.

Glossary

blockades (blah-KAYDS) Ships that block passage to ports by ships of another country.

Congress (KON-gres) The part of the U.S. government that makes laws.

declaration of war (deh-kluh-RAY-shun UV WUR) A written notice calling for war of one nation with another.

economy (ih-KAH-nuh-mee) A country's ability to make products, sell them, and earn money.

merchant shipping (MER-chant SHIP-ing) Cargo ships that take products to foreign markets.

piracy (PY-rih-see) The act of attacking and robbing ships.

reinforcement (ree-in-FORS-ment) Anything that strengthens, specifically additional troops or warships to make stronger those already sent.

retreat (ree-TREET) Leaving the scene of battle because of its danger.

revolution (reh-vuh-LOO-shun) A complete change in government.

Revolutionary War (reh-vuh-LOO-shuh-ner-ee WOR) The war between the colonies and Great Britain that resulted in the United States becoming its own country.

surrender (suh-REN-der) To give up.

territory (TER-uh-tor-ee) Land that is controlled by a person or a group of people.

treaty (TREE-tee) A written agreement to do something, such as to stop fighting a war.

Web Sites

Due to the changing nature of Internet links, the Rosen Publishing Group, Inc., has developed an online list of Web sites related to the subject of this book. This site is updated regularly. Please use this link to access the list:

http://www.rosenlinks.com/lnan/waei

Primary Source Image List

Page 1: Monograph by Samuel R. Brown. Created in 1815. Housed in a collection of Filson Library.

Page 5: Print by John Baker. Created in 1882. Housed in the National Archives and Records Administration.

Page 6: Portrait by Jacques-Louis David. Created in 1812.

Page 9: Drawing by Wade. Created in 1855. Housed in the Healy Collection.

Page 12: Portrait by Henry Bryan Hall. Created in 1860. Housed in the Stapleton Collection at the Indiana University of Pennsylvania.

Page 15: Print entitled "Camp at Detroit." Created on August 16, 1812. Housed at the National Archives and Records Administration.

Page 16: Lithograph by N. Carony. Housed in the collection of Nathaniel Currier.

Page 18: Portrait by Gilbert Stuart. Created in 1821. Housed at the National Gallery of Art, Washington, D.C.

Page 20: Engraving by G. Thompson. Created in October 14, 1814.

Page 23 (top): The Treaty of Ghent, signed on December 24, 1814. Housed in the National Archives and Records Administration.

Page 23 (bottom): Painting created on December 21, 1814. Housed in the National Archives and Records Administration.

Page 24: Engraving by H. B. Hall after a W. Monberger original. Created in 1815. Housed in the National Archives and Records Administration.

Page 26: Print by William Charles. Created in 1813.

Index

About the Author

Mark Beyer has written more than fifty children's and young adult nonfiction books. He lives outside New York City.